Written by Laurence Anholt
Illustrated by Arthur Robins

ORCHARD BOOKS
338 Euston Road, London NW1 3BH
Orchard Books Australia
Level 17/207 Kent Street, Sydney, NSW 2000

First published in Great Britain by Orchard Books: *Cinderboy* 1996, *The Fried Piper of Hamstring* 1998 and *Ghostyshocks and the Three Scares* 2000.
This bind-up edition first published in 2012.

A Paperback Original

ISBN 978 1 40832 420 2

A CIP catalogue record for this book is available from the British Library.

1 3 5 7 9 10 8 6 4 2

Printed in Great Britain

Orchard Books is a division of Hachette Children's Books,
an Hachette UK company

SP[illegible]ALL THE SERIOUSLY SILLY PEO[illegible]

SERIOUSLY SILLY STORYLAND

DARE TO BE BARE

Tra la-la!

☆ The Fried Piper ☆ Shampoozel ☆ Daft Jack ☆ The Emperor ☆
☆ Little Red Riding Wolf ☆ Rumply Crumply Stinky Pin ☆

☆ Ghostyshocks ☆ Snow White ☆ Cinderboy ☆ Eco-Wolf ☆
☆ The Greedy Farmer ☆ Billy Beast ☆

CINDERBOY

Cinderboy was crazy about football.

His wicked stepdad and his two lazy stepbrothers were football crazy too. The whole family supported Royal Palace United.

Royal Palace are MA-AGIC
Everyone else is TRA-AGIC!
FOOTBALL

Every Saturday they would lie about on the sofa with the remote control and watch their favourite team on TV. Royal Palace always played brilliantly in their smart pink shorts and shirts.

But not poor Cinderboy. He wasn't even allowed to watch. He had to wait on his stepbrothers hand and foot, and bring them cups of tea and bowl after bowl of peanuts, which were their favourite snack.

Cinderboy's family was very noisy and bad mannered. When Royal Palace scored they would jump up and down on the sofa and shout for more peanuts to celebrate.

And when the other team scored they would throw their peanuts at the TV, then yell at Cinderboy to pick them up so that they could throw them again.

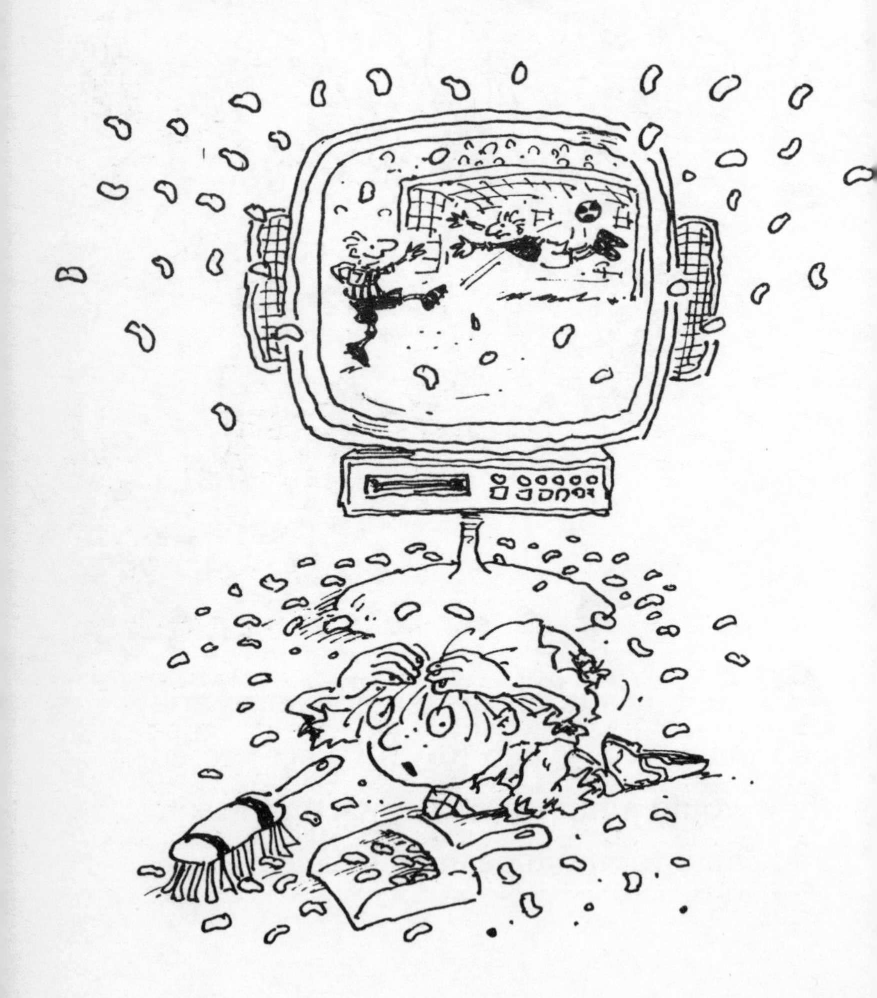

One day his cruel stepfather said to Cinderboy, "Listen, Cinders, tomorrow is the day of the big Cup Final. I am taking your stepbrothers to the Royal Palace stadium to watch the match. And while we are gone you must clean the whole house from top to bottom."

"Yes," said his stepbrothers, "we want every last peanut picked up from under the sofa."

Poor Cinderboy was very unhappy. He would have loved to see his team play in the Cup Final more than anything else in the world.

The next morning he had to wake up earlier than ever to prepare peanut butter sandwiches for his horrible brothers who only laughed at the tears in Cinder's eyes.

As they drove away, shouting and tooting the horn, Cinderboy lay on the sofa and cried and cried and cried.

Then he had an idea. He would work as hard as anything to clean the house so that he could watch the big Cup Final on TV.

He set to work straight away

. . . scrubbing his stepbrothers' smelly football socks

. . . and hoovering up every last peanut from under the sofa.

When at last the work was done, the house sparkled from top to bottom.

Cinderboy pulled up his little stool, found the remote control and switched on the TV.

ROYAL PALACE ARE MA-AGIC!
EVERYONE ELSE IS TRA-AGIC!

The match had just begun. The terraces were packed with cheering Royal Palace fans. Cinderboy even caught a glimpse of his stepfather and brothers sitting in the front row, waving their pink scarves and throwing peanuts at the referee.

Oh, how Cinderboy wished he could go to a real live football match!

What made him feel even sadder was that Royal Palace were not playing well that day. Soon the other side had scored and Cinderboy felt sadder than ever.

To make matters worse, just before half-time a terrible thing happened – the Royal Palace captain was kicked in the shin and had to be carried off the field on a stretcher.

When the half-time whistle blew, Royal Palace were ten–nil down and struggling without their best player.

During the advertisements Cinderboy was crying so hard he could hardly see the television.

Suddenly, a pink face appeared on the TV screen before him.

"Don't cry, Cindy," it said.

Cinderboy rubbed his eyes. "There must be something wrong with the television," he thought. The face seemed to be talking to *him!*

"Who . . . who . . . who are you?" he stuttered.

"I am your TV Godmother," said the face on the television. "And guess what, Cindy? You *shall* go to the big Cup Final!"

"But I don't have anything to wear," stammered Cinderboy.

"Don't worry, Cinderboy. Just press button 13 on the remote control," said the TV Godmother.

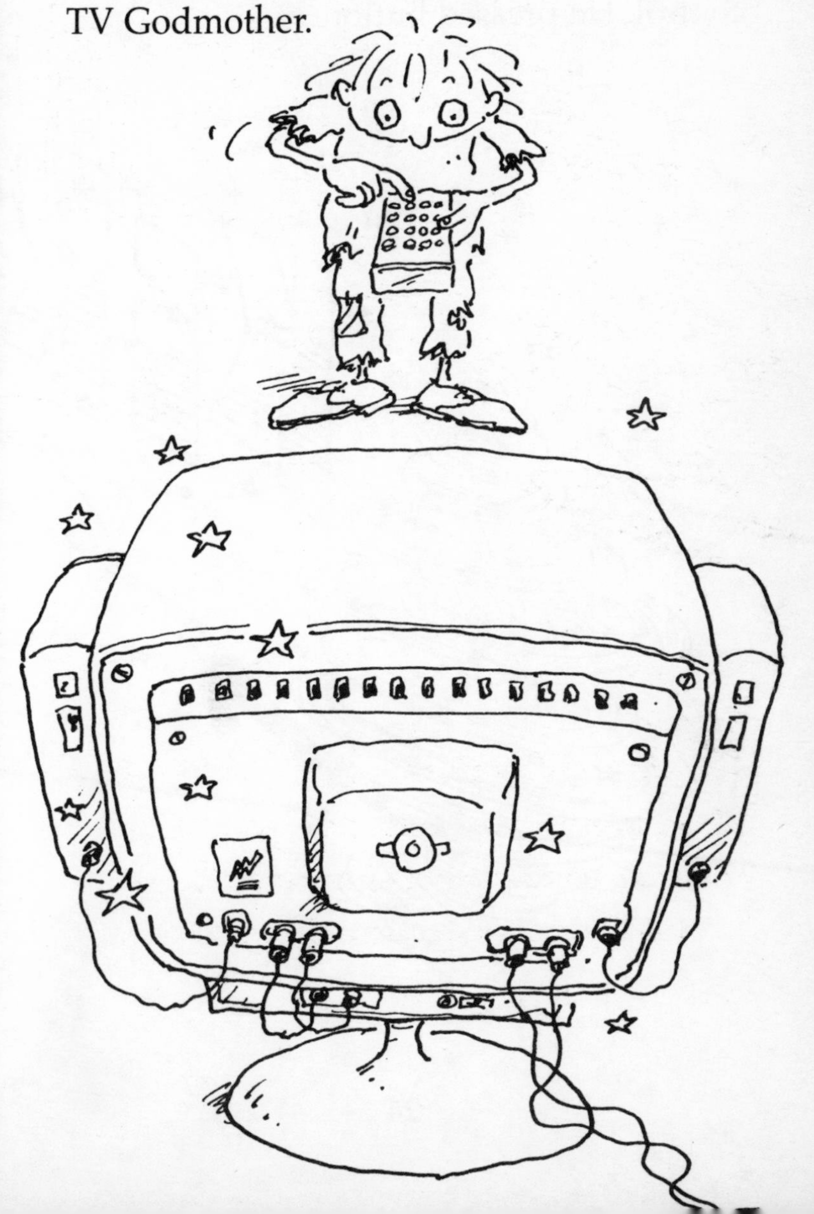

Cinderboy wiped his eyes with the back of his hand and held out the remote control. He pressed button 13.

As if by magic the scruffy old clothes he was wearing disappeared – and Cinderboy stood tall and handsome, dressed in a pink silk shirt and pink silk shorts. On his feet were a pair of brand new football boots with gleaming glass studs.

"Oh, thank you, TV Godmother! But. . . how will I get to the big Cup Final?"

"Oooh, you are a big worrier!" said the voice from the TV. "Press button 14 on the remote control."

Cinderboy pressed button 14.

As if by magic the old sofa changed into a long shiny pink limousine with a pink uniformed chauffeur at the wheel.

"Oh, thank you! Thank you!" cried Cinderboy.

"Just one thing, Cindy doll," said the face on TV, "no one must recognise you. Wear this mask at all times."

A hand reached out of the screen holding a pink silk mask. "And most important of all, you must return home before the referee blows the final whistle."

Without a second thought, Cinderboy grabbed the mask and jumped into the limousine and roared out through the door.

It seemed like only seconds before he screeched to a halt in the stadium car park.

Cinderboy pulled on the pink mask and ran towards a big open door. When he looked around, he was standing . . .

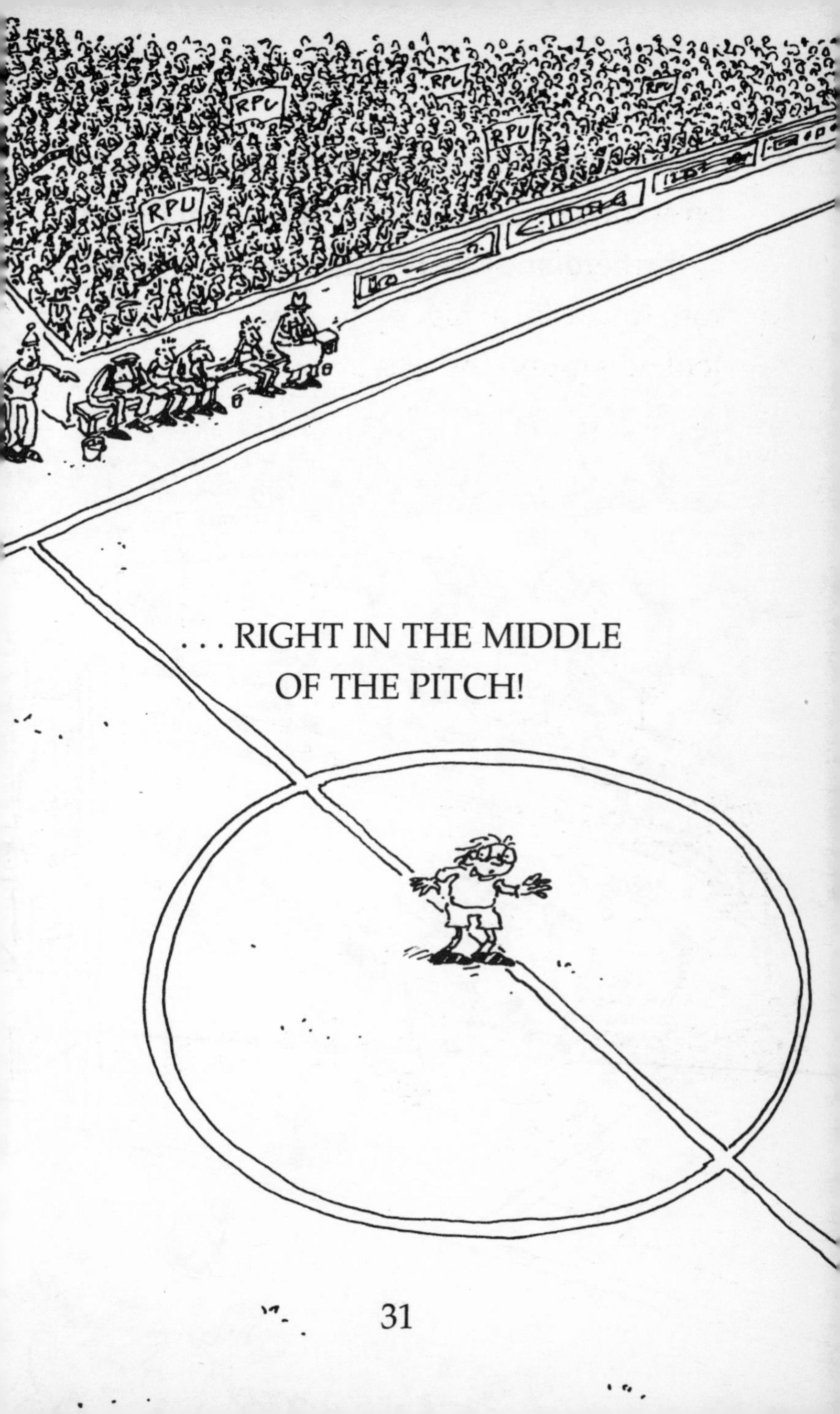

. . . RIGHT IN THE MIDDLE
OF THE PITCH!

The crowd cheered in excitement as the mysterious pink-masked player charged on to the field and headed straight for the ball.

He skilfully tackled the other players, flicking the ball into the air with his left foot and sprinting towards the goal post. Then, to the amazement of the Royal Palace fans – KERBAM! He shot it into the back of the net!

The crowd went wild.

Only ten more minutes to go. Cinderboy manoeuvred the ball around the pitch as gracefully as a dancer at a fairy-tale ball.

Then – KERBOOM! Cinderboy scored again. And – KERBLAM! He headed the ball into the back of the net.

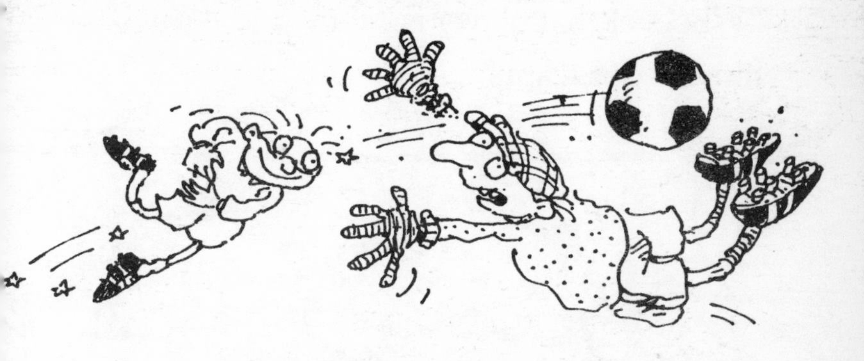

KERWOOMPH! He bounced it into the goal with the tip of his glass-studded boot. The stadium roared with applause.

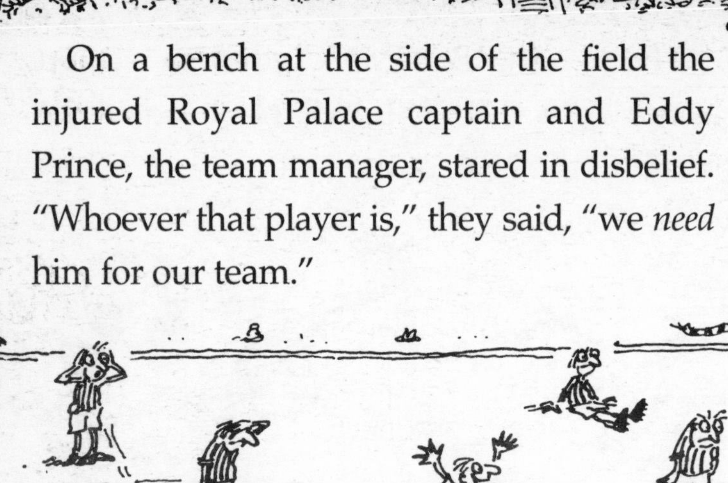

On a bench at the side of the field the injured Royal Palace captain and Eddy Prince, the team manager, stared in disbelief. "Whoever that player is," they said, "we *need* him for our team."

Before long, the score was equal – ten all. But soon there were only seconds left to play and the ball was at the wrong end of the field.

Cinderboy noticed the referee put the whistle to his lips.

"TV Godmother, help me!" he whispered.

One last time Cinderboy dived towards the ball. With a mighty swing he kicked it so hard that one of his glass-studded boots flew off and then tumbled to the ground.

The ball shot upwards like a rocket. The whole crowd rose to their feet.

The rival team stood open-mouthed as the ball soared like a bird through the sky. At the other end of the field it began to fall. It bounced once, then dropped effortlessly into the centre of the net.

RPU
11
GIANTS
10
6

Royal Palace had won the Cup Final! The crowd went ballistic! A thousand pink caps were thrown into the air. Eddy Prince raced on to the pitch to sign up the mystery player.

But Cinderboy, remembering the promise to his TV Godmother, ran out of the stadium as fast as his one boot would carry him.

But, to his dismay, when he reached the car park, he found only the battered old sofa where the pink limousine had been.

And poor old Cinderboy had to push the sofa home.

The man in the pink mask was fantastic
Royal Palace were MA-AGIC!
The rest of the world is TRA-AGIC!

"You should have seen him!" shouted the stepbrothers when they finally returned home from the celebrations.

"Yeah!" they smirked, "and poor old Cinderboy missed the whole thing."

Cinderboy only smiled to himself. That night, as he lay in his broken old bed, tears of joy sparkled in his eyes as he dreamed about the day he had scored the winning goal for Royal Palace United, the best team in the whole wide world.

Early the next morning there was a knock at the door. Cinderboy ran to answer it. He couldn't believe his eyes! There stood Eddy Prince, the Royal Palace manager.

"I'm searching for the mysterious boy in the pink mask," he said. "The person who fits this gleaming glass-studded boot will play for the Royal Palace team for the rest of their days."

"Oooh!" said the lazy stepbrothers, coming downstairs in their pyjamas. "Let me try! Let me try! It's no good asking Cinderboy – he didn't even watch the match! Go and fetch some peanuts for Mr Prince, Cinders."

The first greedy stepbrother snatched the glass-studded boot from Eddy Prince.

He tore off his slipper and shoved his sweaty foot into the boot. But no matter how hard he pushed, he couldn't get the boot on.

Then the second greedy stepbrother stepped forward and grabbed the boot.

His foot was slightly smaller and slightly sweatier. He shoved . . .

and squeezed . . .

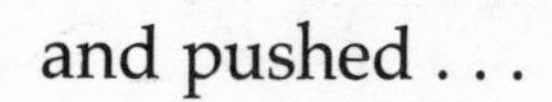

and pushed . . .

and heaved . . .

and suddenly – PLOP! His foot was inside.

"IT FITS! IT FITS!" he shouted. "Father, Father, come and look! I'm going to play for Royal Palace!
I'm going to be on telly!
I'm going to be rich!
I'm going to buy a peanut factory . . .

Everyone's going to cheer, just like they did for the boy in the pink mask – I mean *me*, of course."

"Oh!" said Eddy Prince, looking a little surprised. "Are you sure it was you? I'm afraid you'll have to do a little training . . ."

Suddenly Cinderboy stepped out of the kitchen.

On his face he wore . . . a pink silk mask!

In his hand was . . . a tiny pair of pink shorts!

"Well then, stepbrother," he said. "Let's see you fit into *these* . . ." And he held out the pink shorts.

Everyone gasped. But try as he might, his stepbrother had eaten too many peanuts to squeeze into the shorts.

So Cinderboy drove away with Eddy Prince to begin a new life as Royal Palace's star player.

But being a kind sort of boy, he soon forgave his wicked stepfather and his greedy brothers and arranged for them to have as many free tickets as they wanted to see Royal Palace play.

He even offered to pay for the operation to have the glass-studded boot removed from his stepbrother's foot.

And Cinderboy lived happily ever after, and scored more goals for Royal Palace than there are peanuts under all the sofas in the whole wide world.

THE FRIED PIPER of HAMSTRING

The grown-ups in Hamstring Town were the bossiest people in the ENTIRE UNIVERSE.

They would never leave
their kids alone . . .

Nag nag nag.
Do this.
Don't do that.
Wash your hair.
Eat your greens.
Go to sleep.

It never ever stopped.

The grown-ups had rules for everything. Every child had to know them by heart:

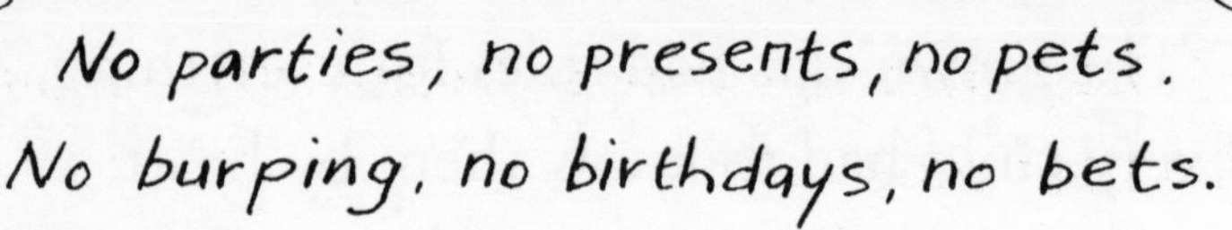

No skipping, no spitting, no sun...
No football, no fried food...
... NO FUN!

The grown-ups were especially strict about the fried food.

"All those greasy chips and hamburgers will give you spots and make you lazy," they would tell their little ones.

So the poor children of Hamstring were allowed only organic fruit and vegetables, three times a day, and NO snacks between meals.

Everything in Hamstring Town was spick and span. Little girls had shiny hair in pretty bows. Boys wore short trousers until their thirty-fifth birthday, even if their legs were hairy. In the evening, families had spelling tests together.

It was boring.
It was gloomy.
It was DULL!

But, of all the bossy grown-ups in Hamstring Town, no one was stricter than the Mayor.

The Mayor of Hamstring spent all his time inventing new rules to make things even tidier. He didn't like children and he especially hated animals.

"Animals are so messy," he would snarl. "Let's have a new law. From now on, all cows must be toilet trained.

"And BIRDS . . ." he shouted ". . . birds are dirty little creatures. From today all birds must wear nappies."

The boys and girls of Hamstring would have given anything for their own little puppy or a baby hamster or even a stick insect, but pets were strictly forbidden in Hamstring Town.

As the days passed, things got worse and worse.

On Monday the Mayor banned music, moustaches and morris men.

On Tuesday he banned chewing gum, chocolate and chattering.

On Wednesday he banned watches, weeds and whispering.

On Thursday he banned theatres, thunderstorms and thinking.

On Friday he banned freckles, frogs and fireworks.

On Saturday he banned scratching, scarecrows and smiling.

On Sunday – well, on Sunday some of the children sneaked off to meet secretly.

"This has gone too far," whispered one of the big children. "Soon there will be nothing left to ban. We must do something NOW. We must stop that mad Mayor."

"We need some help," said a little girl at the back.

"Yes," said a boy. "We need a person who isn't afraid of grown-ups."

So the children typed out a secret message. It said:

> S.O.S.
> Hamstring kids urgently require
> A FEARLESS HERO
> to save the town
> from a power-mad mayor
> and too many RULES!
> HELP! Come quick.

The children sent the message out to every newspaper in the land.

They sent it by e-mail. They faxed it. They posted it on-line. 'Replies to: www.rulebuster@hamstring.com'

Then they went home for tea.

At first light, as the children wandered wearily to school, they spotted a strange figure high on a mountain top above the town.

The children could tell straight away that the stranger was not from their town because he was dressed in the most extraordinary way.

Instead of grey shorts, he wore red and yellow jeans and a bomber jacket to match. His hair was tied in a ponytail; a gleaming gold saxophone hung round his neck. Most outrageous of all, the boy was sitting on a dazzling mountain bike.

To the children's amazement, the stranger leapt on to the saddle and hurtled down the hillside to where they were standing.

In a great cloud of dust, the bike spun to a halt.

It was only then that the children realised the stranger was holding something in his gloved hands . . .

Something terrible . . . Something so wicked, it was banned throughout all Hamstring . . .

. . . A Mega-Burger with French Fries, all sprinkled with salt and dripping with tomato ketchup!

A gasp ran through the crowd.

The children stared wide-eyed as the boy began to speak in strange musical words:

"I was out on my bike, just takin' a cruise,
I nearly freaked out when I heard the news.

"Said, 'I'll hit the road and burn on down,
To help those dudes in Hamstring Town.'

"Yeah, I'm the Fried Piper and I am hip,
Any of you cool cats care for...A CHIP?"

The children of Hamstring stood frozen. They couldn't believe their eyes.

Then, very slowly, a tiny boy stepped forward. He looked around, and, quick as a flash, he grabbed a chip from the Fried Piper's outstretched hand and stuffed it into his mouth.

It was the first chip he had ever eaten. And it was DELICIOUS!

In a second, everyone had gathered round, stuffing chips into their mouths, laughing and chattering and admiring the beautiful bike.

"But . . . but are you really allowed a bike?" someone asked. "What about The Rules?"

The Fried Piper only laughed and tossed back his golden hair.

"You know, rules ain't cool. I do what I like,
I dig fried food and I LOVE my bike.

"If you follow me, then pretty soon,
You'll hear me blowin' a RADICAL tune!"

The children knew they should be at school, but somehow, they couldn't help it. They *had* to follow that wonderful smell of fried chips and tomato sauce. The Fried Piper led them slowly down the road towards the centre of Hamstring Town.

At that moment, the wicked Mayor was searching for children who were late for school. Suddenly he heard an unusual noise. It sounded like scurrying feet. It sounded like chattering. It sounded like laughing. It sounded like . . . CHILDREN!

The Mayor spun around.

"ARE YOU MAD?" he shouted. "This is SCHOOL TIME. Have you forgotten Rule 48B, Subsection 19? It clearly says that any child absent from school for any reason shall . . ."

The Mayor stopped. He stared. His jaw hung open. The Fried Piper stepped out of the crowd. He pushed his bike into the town square, where the sun cast long shadows . . .

"HEY! You Mayor. You big fat dude,
We don't dig your rules, we don't dig your food.

"You got too much belly and not enough hair,
You're what I call a real NIGHT MAYOR!"

The children began to laugh. They just couldn't stop.

The Mayor struggled for something to say. He turned red. The children laughed more.

At last the Mayor blurted out, "THIS . . . THIS IS AN OUTRAGE! Where are your shorts, young man? There are rules . . . RULES . . . RULES!!"

Slowly,
the Fried Piper
stepped forward.
He leaned his bike
carefully against a railing. His long fingers drummed on his saxophone. His dark eyes fixed on the Mayor. A strange silence fell over the town.

In a firm, low voice the stranger whispered,

"Chill out, Mayor. That's enough of your threats,
Us kids need fun and we need...PETS!"

At the sound of the word 'pets', the Mayor gasped.

The Piper put his gleaming gold instrument to his lips and began to play – a weird haunting tune which rose up above the houses and all across the mountains around Hamstring Town.

Everyone stood in silence, until they heard a faint, distant squeaking. To the Mayor's horror, a tiny baby rat came scampering along the main street, sniffing the air and twitching its little whiskers.

The rat was followed by a guinea pig. The guinea pig by a hamster. Behind the hamster bounced two long-eared rabbits. The rabbits were followed by kittens. The kittens by puppies.

And still the Piper played on.

The children of Hamstring scooped up the little animals and started to stroke and kiss them.

The Mayor began to shake.
"The Rules," he croaked. "The Rules . . ."
But the Fried Piper didn't miss a note.

More and more pets came hopping and bounding into the main square of Hamstring. Big and small. Tortoises, budgies, ponies. Parrots, dogs, cats. Squeaking, yapping, barking. Whistling, grunting, yelping.

The children were delighted. They ran to meet the new animals who jumped up and licked their happy faces. Behind the noise, the strange tune continued.

Donkeys, goats, monkeys. Lizards, lambs, frogs. Rolling, running, racing. Scurrying, scampering, chasing.

A large dog licked the Mayor's ear. A monkey climbed onto his hat. The Mayor put his hands to his face and began to weep.

"The Rules," he sobbed. "Oh, the Rules . . ."

The bossy grown-ups of Hamstring had been watching their children in dismay. Now they turned and ran. Down the street and out of the town. Over the mountains and far far away.

Only one person could not keep up. The Mayor ran as fast as his fat little legs would carry him, but as he reached the edge of the mountains, a huge kangaroo bounded after him.

She scooped him up and shoved him into her pouch.

As they bounded back to town, the Mayor squealed, "NO KANGAROOS! NO HOPPING! NO BOUNCING!"

That evening, there was great feasting in Hamstring. The children lit a fire in the town square and the Mayor was made to cook the most enormous fry-up of all time: fried eggs, fried bread, fried bananas and - most of all - hundreds and thousands of chips, dripping in tomato sauce.

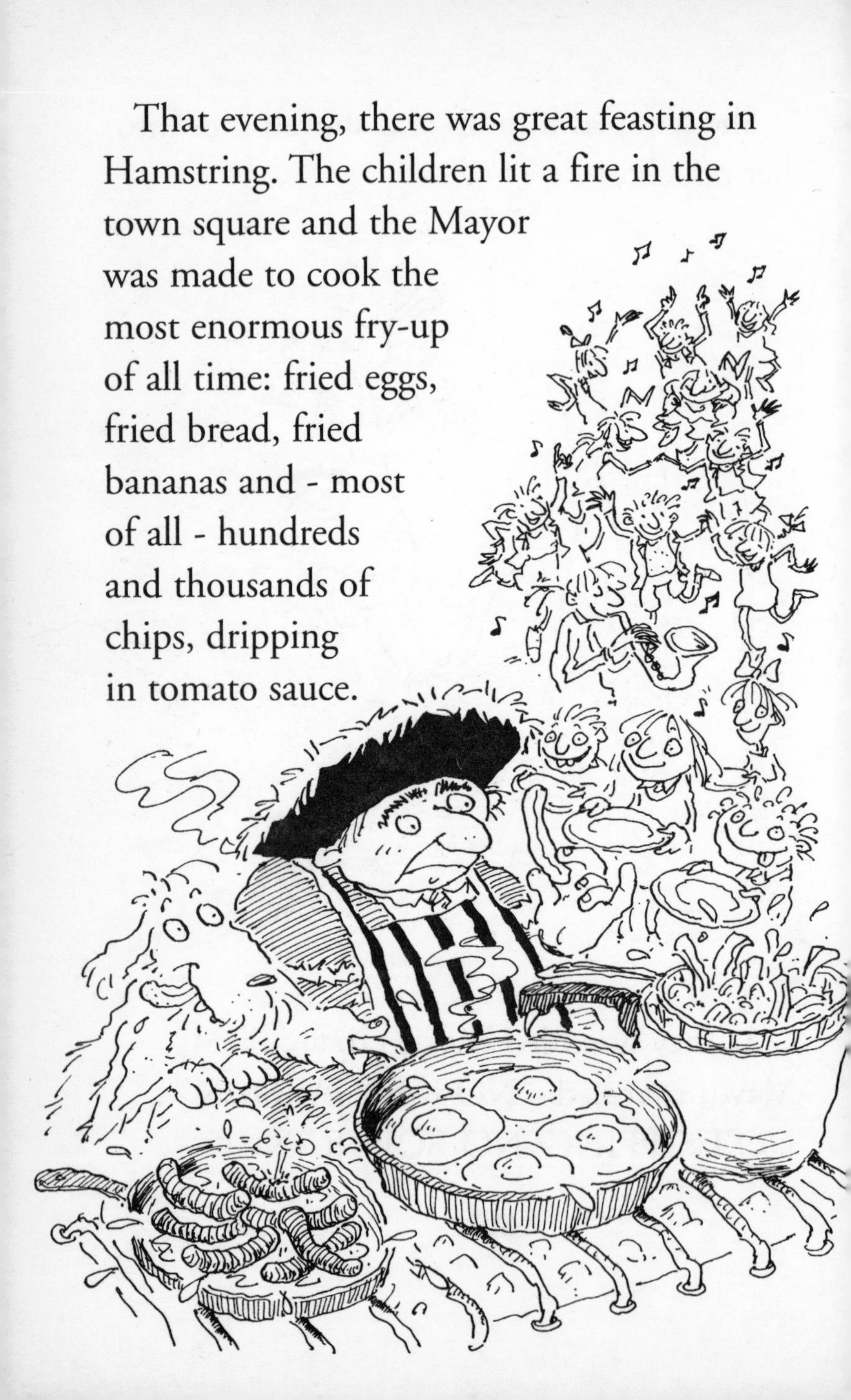

Late into the night, the children and their pets danced to the wild tunes of the Fried Piper.

The party lasted four long days. When it was over, the grown-ups crept quietly home from their hiding places in the mountains.

The Mayor was still busy cleaning the frying pan.

So the Fried Piper made one or two rules of his own.

Gather round dudes, here's my number one rule:
Think for yourself and you'll always be cool.
Like what you do and do what you like.
Hey! Anyone seen my mountain bike?

And the Fried Piper rode away into the sunset.

To this very day there are no rules in Hamstring town. The people do exactly what they please. They are the coolest cats for miles around.

And the hippest, smoothest, most radical dude of them all is . . .

. . . that crazy old Mayor himself.

GHOSTYSHOCKS and the THREE SCARES

It was a dark and stormy night. Three bears were moving into an old house in a spooky forest.

Their terrible howls echoed through the trees and terrified the people of the nearby village.

There was a huge hairy Daddy Bear howl: "WOOO-HOOOOO!"

A middle-sized Mummy Bear howl:
"Yoo-hoo!"

And a terrible teeny-weeny Baby Bear howl: "Wheee!"

The more the villagers heard, the more nervous they became. A story went around that their new neighbours were VAMPIRE BEARS!

The people of the village refused to go near the forest, and visitors would find them pale and trembling.

There was one girl who was more afraid than anyone. The slightest squeak made her jump. Even the tiniest spider made her SCREAM!

When anyone asked her name, she would reply:

It's G-G-G...
Glenda Gobstopper?
NO. G-G-G...
Good King Wenceslas?
NO. G-G-G...

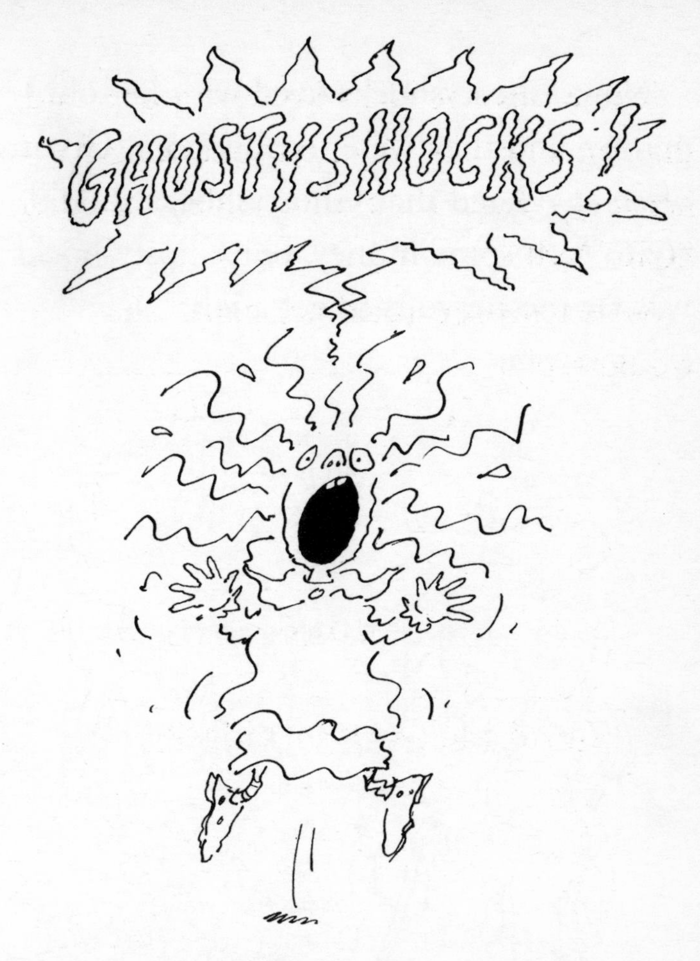

Two things frightened Ghostyshocks more than anything else in the world. The first was the dark, dangerous forest, and the second was . . . VAMPIRE BEARS!

Now, Ghostyshocks lived with her old granny, and they were terribly poor. Granny often suggested that Ghostyshocks should try to earn some money, but Ghostyshocks was far too nervous to get a job.

"Couldn't you do a little baby-sitting, dear?" her granny would ask.

One foggy winter's day, Ghostyshocks's granny was in bed with a bad cold.

"Ghostyshocks, the fire has gone out," she said. "You must go out to collect more wood."

Ghostyshocks went pale. There was only one place to collect wood...

"I'm sorry, Ghostyshocks," said her granny, "But you're a big girl now, and the house is cold."

And so it was that Ghostyshocks crept outside, trembling from top-to-toe.

She climbed the little path from the village, and entered the creepy black forest.

At that very moment, the three bears were waking up.

Daddy Bear yawned a huge daddy-sized yawn: "WOOO-HOOOOO!"

Mummy Bear yawned a middle-sized yawn: "Yoo-hoo!"

And teeny-weeny Baby Bear yawned a teeny-weeny baby-sized yawn: "Wheee!"

Down in the village, every door and window banged shut.

Deep in the forest, poor Ghostyshocks huddled beneath a blueberry bush.

In their new house, the three bears got dressed and went downstairs.

Mummy Bear poured out their breakfast. It looked delicious – bright red and steaming!

A big red bowlful for Daddy Bear. A middle-sized red bowlful for Mummy Bear. And a teeny-weeny red bowlful for Baby Bear.

But – oh dear! – their breakfast was far too hot.

Daddy Bear burnt his tongue, and howled a HUGE Daddy Bear howl: "WOOO-HOOOOO!"

Mummy Bear burnt her tongue, and howled a middle-sized howl: "Yoo-hoo!"

And teeny-weeny Baby Bear burnt his tongue, and howled a teeny-weeny baby-sized howl: "Wheee!"

Down in the village, everyone crawled under their tables and beds, and hugged each other in fear.

Deep, deep in the darkest part of the dark and dangerous forest, Ghostyshocks was as jittery as a jellyfish.

She ran off the path and hid in the undergrowth.

"Why are you out all alone?" asked a deer.

At the bears' house, Daddy Bear said, "*Oooh*, this breakfast is far too hot, Mummy Bear. I'll tell you what, let's have a nice walk while it cools off. Come on, Baby Bear, grab your wellies."

So the three bears put on their boots, and went out into the forest for a stroll.

By now, Ghostyshocks had wandered further and further from the path. Twigs scratched at her face like wicked witches' fingers. To her horror, she realised that she was completely lost.

So Ghostyshocks stumbled up to the huge black door, and with a shaky finger rang the bell. No one answered, but the door slowly creaked open. *CRE-E-EAK!*

Ghostyshocks stepped inside. Her stomach felt knotted like knitted knickers, and her knees were knocking nervously.

Before her was a large table. Three places were set for breakfast. There was a big bowl, a middle-sized bowl, and a teeny-weeny baby bowl.

But what was *inside* the bowls?

Ghostyshocks dipped her finger into the big bowl. "*Uuurgh!*" she gasped. "It's d-d-disgusting!"

She dipped a finger into the middle-sized bowl. "W-w-what *is* it?"

She picked up the teeny-weeny baby bowl, and stared at the red liquid inside.

She remembered the terrible stories of vampire bears, and suddenly she shrieked, "It must be BL-BL-BLOOD!"

Ghostyshocks was shaking so much that she spilt the whole bowl all down her clean dress.

"EEEEEEEEEKK!" she screamed.

She had to sit down before she fainted with fright.

She found a huge
chair, but it was
far too big.

She found
a middle-sized
chair, but that
was too hard.

She found
a teeny-weeny
baby-sized high-chair
and that was too small,
but she sat in it anyway.

The teeny-weeny high-chair shattered into teeny-tiny pieces.

"Aaargh!" screamed Ghostyshocks, and she ran out and up the twisting staircase.

Gasping for breath, she stumbled into a bedroom. Then, to her horror, Ghostyshocks heard voices downstairs:

"HOI! Somebody's been poking their paws in my breakfast!" roared a huge, great voice.

"And somebody's been playing with my breakfast. How unhygienic," said a middle-sized voice.

"And somebody's been mucking about with my breakfast," said a teeny-weeny voice, "and spilt the whole bowl."

Ghostyshocks searched desperately for a place to hide. She pulled back the covers on a huge bed, but they'd easily spot her in there.

She tried to hide in the middle-sized bed, but the bears would look there too.

Then Ghostyshocks noticed a teeny-weeny bed, in the far corner of the room. She crawled inside and pulled the sheets right over her head.

"Hoi! Somebody's been sitting in my chair!" roared a huge, great voice downstairs.

"And somebody's been sitting in my chair," said a middle-sized voice.

"And somebody's been sitting in my chair," said a teeny-weeny voice, "and they've smashed it into teeny-tiny pieces."

Ghostyshocks heard footsteps creaking up the stairs, and coming slowly along the dark corridor.

They came closer . . .

and closer . . .

and *closer!*

The door was slowly pushed open . . .

"Somebody's been lying in my bed!" roared a huge, great voice.

"And somebody's been lying in my bed," said a middle-sized voice.

Ghostyshocks closed her eyes as tight as she could, and lay frozen with fear. She heard the loud breathing of the bears as they searched the room. Closer...and closer...and *closer!*

Suddenly, a hairy paw grabbed the blankets on the teeny-weeny bed, and tore them away.

The three bears stared at Ghostyshocks. She was as white as a sheet and covered with a ghastly red stain.

"Somebody's been bumped-off in my bed," squeaked a teeny-weeny voice, "and *she's still there!*"

"WOOO-HOOOOO!" screamed the big Daddy Bear.

"Yoo-hoo!" yelled the middle-sized Mummy Bear.

"Wheee!" squealed the teeny-weeny Baby Bear.

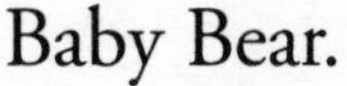

The three bears were terrified. They turned and ran for the door.

"W-w-wait," said Ghostyshocks, sitting up in bed.

"Promise you won't hurt me," said the teeny-weeny Baby Bear.

"Of c-c-course I won't," said Ghostyshocks.

"Well, let's all go downstairs and have some breakfast," said Mummy Bear. "I've made some lovely tomato soup, and I'm sure it's cool now."

"Tomato soup?" said Ghostyshocks. "Does that mean you're not v-v-v . . . ? I thought you were v-v-v . . . ?"

"Vegetarians, dear? Of course we are. Daddy Bear grows all our own vegetables."

So the three bears and Ghostyshocks had breakfast together.

Mummy Bear washed Ghostyshocks's dress, and Daddy Bear said it didn't matter at all about the teeny-weeny high-chair because Baby Bear was getting quite big now. He put all the pieces of wood into Ghostyshocks's bag for firewood.

"We must come down and meet your granny and everyone in the village," said Mummy Bear. "We wanted to visit, only we don't like leaving little Baby Bear."

"I'm the best baby-sitter for miles around," said Ghostyshocks. "Three pounds an hour. Four pounds at weekends. You provide tea, coffee and snacks . . . and easy on the tomato soup."

"But wouldn't you be nervous, out here with just Baby Bear?" asked Daddy Bear.

"Who me?" said Ghostyshocks, "Nothing scares me. We'll play in the forest, and tell each other ghost stories . . ."

...It'll be an absolute scream!

Max and Molly's Guide To Trouble!

Meet Max and Molly: terrorising the neighbourhood really extremely politely...

Max and Molly's guides guarantee brilliantly funny mayhem and mischief as we learn how to be a genius, catch a criminal, build an abominable snowman and stop a Viking invasion!

978 1 40830 519 5 £4.99 Pbk
978 1 40831 572 9 eBook

978 1 40830 520 1 £4.99 Pbk
978 1 40831 573 6 eBook

978 1 40830 521 8 £4.99 Pbk
978 1 408 31574 3 eBook

978 1 40830 522 5 £4.99 Pbk
978 1 408 31575 0 eBook

ORCHARD BOOKS

www.orchardbooks.co.uk